For Izzy, with thanks

First American Edition 2017
Kane Miller, A Division of EDC Publishing

First published in Great Britain in 2016 by Hodder and Stoughton
Text and illustrations copyright © David Melling 2016
The moral rights of the author have been asserted.
All rights reserved.

For information contact:
Kane Miller, A Division of EDC Publishing
PO Box 470663
Tulsa, OK 74147-0663
www.kanemiller.com
www.edcpub.com
www.usbornebooksandmore.com

Library of Congress Control Number: 2016935529

Printed in China
1 2 3 4 5 6 7 8 9 10

ISBN: 978-1-61067-580-2

D is for Duck!

(and)

David Melling

Kane Miller
A DIVISION OF EDC PUBLISHING

Bunny

Chicken

Duck

Fox

Goat

Hatch

Insects

Jungle

King Lion

Panic

Quick

(Quack)

Run!

up

Vanish!

Where is
everyone?

X (Kiss)

Yuck

DUCK!